WORKING

ANIMALS

For Elinor

**For a free color catalog describing Gareth Stevens'
list of high-quality books and multimedia programs,
call 1-800-542-2595 (USA) or 1-800-461-9120 (Canada).
Gareth Stevens Publishing's Fax: (414) 225-0377.
See our catalog, too, on the World Wide Web:
http://gsinc.com**

Library of Congress Cataloging-in-Publication Data

Stickland, Paul.
    Animals / Paul Stickland.
      p. cm. — (Working)
    Includes index.
    Summary: Brief text and illustrations enumerate several
animals that help humans, including guide dogs, camels,
elephants, bees, and donkeys.
    ISBN 0-8368-2156-4 (lib. bdg.)
    1. Working animals—Juvenile literature. [1. Working animals.
2. Animals.] I. Title. II. Series: Stickland, Paul. Working.
SF172.S75   1998
636.088'6—dc21   98-15943

This North American edition first published in 1998 by
Gareth Stevens Publishing
1555 North RiverCenter Drive, Suite 201
Milwaukee, Wisconsin 53212 USA

© 1991 by Paul Stickland.
Designed by Herman Lelie.
Produced by Mathew Price Ltd.,
The Old Glove Factory, Bristol Road,
Sherborne, Dorset DT9 4HP, England.
Additional end matter © 1998
by Gareth Stevens, Inc.

Gareth Stevens series editor: Dorothy L. Gibbs
Editorial assistant: Diane Laska

Printed in Hong Kong
1 2 3 4 5 6 7 8 9 02 01 00 99 98

ANIMALS

Paul Stickland

Gareth Stevens Publishing
MILWAUKEE

Camels carry heavy loads.
They can make long trips across
the scorching desert without water.

4

Bees collect nectar from flowers and
make it into honey in their hives.

6

Blind people trust their guide dogs to
lead them safely wherever they go.

Indian elephants can clear away huge
logs without damaging other trees.

8

They are better than tractors!

Donkeys are very strong. They can
carry heavy loads a long way.

A sheepdog rounds up the flock when
it hears the farmer whistle.

A cowboy's horse is fast and clever.
It catches up easily with runaway cattle.

Some farms have lots of cats. They are
good pets and can also be very useful.

Cats catch hungry mice and rats that
eat the farmer's corn.

GLOSSARY

blind — not able to see.

cattle — animals, such as cows and bulls, that are found on farms and ranches.

clever — able to think and move quickly and correctly.

damaging — causing a loss by harming or injuring something.

nectar — the sweet liquid in flowers that bees use to make honey.

runaway — something running away or escaping from where it belongs.

scorching — very hot; hot enough to dry up something or cause a burn.

INDEX